Forbidden Pleasures

Interracial Romance

Taken By My Young Black Student

Everlette Saunders

© 2015

D1522068

Table of Contents:

Chapter 1: Marcus Daniels

Being a traveling lecturer wasn't always my dream, per se, it kind of just fell into my lap. Literally. A few years ago, I was a struggling doctorate student with a shitload of debt slowly piling up. One day, sitting in the cafeteria, a professor of mine shoved a flyer into my hand. It read: "Love your major? Tell the world!" I looked at it, and him, skeptically but put it in my folder anyway. I never expected to give it a second glance, but a few days later it caught my eye as I was rifling through some papers. I got the brochure, sent in my resume, and read up on what it entailed; up until I graduated I would be accompanying other professors on their lectures, maybe saying a few words here and there, all for a stipend. Fuck it, I thought. Some money was better than no money at all.

And now, here I am. Thirty three years old and a traveling lecturer of child psychology. This week, I was lecturing at a small local college. The kids, since they all seemed so much younger than me, were mostly freshmen getting their feet wet in their core classes.

"Okay. Now, I'm sure that you all are somewhat familiar with Erikson's stages of psychosocial development. What, in your opinion, is the most important of the stages in order for one to have a healthy, fruitful life?" I asked, looking around at the lecture hall. A few hands go up, and I call on a young black man sitting towards the back.

"I would say…initiative versus guilt is the most important. That's when, you know, children start to do things on their own and if they don't learn how to do that well, it kind of screws up the rest of their life," he says confidently.

"Very good; very short and to the point. Anyone else?" I continue, but for the rest of my lecture I keep one eye on him. Something about him inexplicably draws me to him, even though he isn't the most handsome thing in the world. His caramel skin glows, and his mouth seems to be twisted in a perpetual smirk, giving him the look of a typical wiseass kid.

My lecture only lasts about an hour, so I'm out of there soon enough. As I stroll down the hallway, I feel a tap on my shoulder. I don't scare too easily, so I coolly turn around…and come face to face with Mr Wiseass from my lecture.

"Oh!" I say in surprise. "Can I help you?"

"Hey, Dr Anderson? I just wanted to tell you I really liked your lecture today. I'm taking Psych 101 this semester so I really needed this because some things just weren't sticking," he chuckles bashfully, his smirk faltering a bit. I smile back, flattered by his words.

"Well, thank you very much, Mr…?" I venture.

"Daniels. Marcus Daniels," he holds out his hand in greeting, and gives me the firmest handshake I've ever experienced. I'm taken aback by this young man and a little bit turned on.

"Well, Mr Daniels, again, thank you. I'll be here for a couple more days, will you be attending my other lectures?"

"Please, call me Marcus. And yes, I believe I will. In fact, I'll make sure I'm there. Like I said, I need this stuff." He fixes his gaze on me, and I'm rendered speechless.

"I'm going down the street for a cup of coffee…would you like to join me?" I offer before I can stop myself. After all, I rationalize, I'm not technically his professor. Somehow, this thought doesn't really settle me, but it gives me enough peace of mind to not stop myself.

"I'd love to," he grins.

Chapter 2: Coffee Date

It's a brisk fall day, but it's still warm enough to get away with just a sweater. Marcus and I walk down the avenue as he picks my brain about different subjects in the vast universe of psychology.

"Now, what about this scenario? A woman of marrying age, who decides to stay at home with her father and rejects any man who tries to start a relationship with her. Would that be, say, her being raised with shame and doubt, since she's obviously refusing to be self-sufficient and using her parent as a safety net, or…?" I shake my head.

"That sounds to me like a case of her Electra complex never having been resolved." We reach the café and order our coffees before taking a seat in a small booth in the corner. "She wants to possess her father sexually, and nobody can really compare to him. Which also is why they say that women look for a partner that is like their father, or, as they say, little girls end up marrying their fathers," I explain.

"I see." Marcus takes a small sip from his steaming latte. "What about you, professor? Do you wish to marry your father?" I blush unintentionally and stir my cappuccino to buy myself some time.

"No, not really," I reply boldly. "I was never much of a daddy's girl; I was always the rebel of my family." He moves so that he's closer to me, close enough that I can smell his aftershave, and I feel my pussy throb.

"Is that so, Dr Anderson?" he murmurs, trailing a hand up my thigh, barely touching my leg, covered in the thin material of my black slacks.

"Absolutely," I whisper hoarsely, now feeling my juices running. "Absolutely," I repeat as he squeezes my thigh. As I move my hand, I accidentally knock my cappuccino over, spilling half of it everywhere. It's not as hot as I thought it was, so it doesn't burn me, but it does make a mess everywhere. "Shit," I mutter as I scramble for the napkins. I run through six of them cleaning the table and seat alone, and my slacks are still sticky.

"Why don't you go clean that off in the bathroom?" Marcus suggests, obviously trying not to laugh at my clumsiness.

"Yeah, looks like I'll have to." I rush to the ladies' room, and luckily there's nobody in there. Sighing sharply, I wet a few paper towels and try to blot as much of the stickiness as I can. Hearing the door swing open behind me makes me turn around, and I'm speechless when I see that it's Marcus. "Marcus, what –" He puts a finger to my lips, shushing me. He pulls me into an empty stall, and I give a quick backwards glance at the door.

"Don't worry about that," he tells me in a sharp but eager tone. I allow him to kiss me, his thick lips almost smothering me, but I like it. He kisses me hard and enthusiastically, and I slide my tongue into his mouth, massaging his with just as much enthusiasm. I feel his hands around my stomach, and I think for a second that he's trying to unbutton my slacks, but he's actually unbuttoning his own jeans. I break the kiss and look down as he pulls out his thick, chocolate cock. "Come wrap those pretty pink lips on this," he tells me.

Chapter 3: Getting Hot and Heavy

Without thinking, I get on my knees and take his whole length into my mouth. I have a hard time getting my mouth around it, so I just take in the tip and suck as I stroke him.

"Get all of it in your mouth, professor," he teases. "Teach me something new." I giggle and open my mouth wider, struggling to fit his girth into my mouth. In the end, I can only take about half of him, but I make sure I give him the sloppiest blowjob possible. Bobbing my head, I simultaneously run my tongue along the underside of his cock, right where the head meets the shaft. I feel it jerk in my mouth and I grip it tighter with my mouth, using as much suction as I can before slowly releasing him.

"I hope you're a quick study," I whisper, looking him straight in the eye with the tip of my tongue teasing the hole in his cock.

"Umm I'll probably need a few more lessons," he bites his bottom lip, making me want to suck them again, but I concentrate on the task at hand. Admiring my new shiny milk chocolate bar, I suck the underside, tugging at the web of skin above his balls and letting them go with a loud sucking noise. "Spit on it," he orders me. "Show me how nasty you head doctors can be." I want to laugh out loud at his attempt at a joke, but the last thing I want is to draw attention to us. As if I had thought it into existence, we hear the door swing open and the click clack of heels. Shit, I whisper to myself, trying to think of what to do. Apparently, Marcus thinks faster than me because he hastily hoists me up to the toilet seat.

"Keep going," he mouths shamelessly. In an awkward crouching position, I open my mouth as wide as I can and engulf as much of his delectable member as possible. He thrusts forward, until I have nearly all of him in my mouth and I gag a bit, trying not to make any noise, which turns him on even more. After what seems like an eternity, I hear Ms. Click Clack wash her hands and leave, and I breathe a sigh of relief, all the while with Marcus still in my mouth. "God, you got a hot mouth, professor." I grab him by his hips, holding him steady while I try to suck his cock as quietly as possible, after our little intrusion. Apparently, I'm doing something right because without warning, he growls and explodes in my mouth. Having no time to react, most of the cum drips out of the corners of my mouth and down my chin. I let go of his cock and lick my lips, savoring the taste and trying to clean off as much as I can.

"I'll see you tomorrow for your next lesson," I tell him, getting up to straighten my clothes and walking out of the bathroom. I glance around to see if anybody noticed me, but the place is so busy that I easily slip out to the street.

Chapter 4: Giving Him The A+

The next day, as I prepare for my lecture my nerves are on edge. I'm almost positive that Marcus will be attending, and I find myself oddly anxious to see him. Since it's a warm day, I have on a sheer blouse, pencil skirt, and black pumps. I sit and wait for everyone to file in, and within fifteen minutes I start the lecture.

"Freud was particularly interested in the body and how it related to different aspects of our sexual growth. Anybody familiar with the first stage?" I ask my captive audience. All the way in the back, Marcus responds before I can call on anybody.

"Oral," he smirks. "It's based on the…pleasure principle." I feel my nipples harden and I have to turn away so that nobody would notice. "It's the beginning of the libidinal gratification in a human being."

"Correct, but please, raise your hand if you want to speak. And that goes for everyone."

"I'm sorry, Dr Anderson," Marcus smiles innocently. I scowl a bit at him, trying to send him a silent warning, but it seems to go unnoticed. Luckily, the rest of my lecture goes smoothly, and everyone participates. My hour goes by quickly, and I'm dismissing my class soon enough. I'm still straightening some papers when out of the corner of my eye I see someone approach. Glancing up, I see Marcus walking towards me, just as the last few students were leaving.

"Yes, Mr Daniels?" I ask in a businesslike tone. "Do you have any questions about today's lecture?"

"No, professor, I actually wanted to bring up another topic, if I may?" I look up to see if anyone else was around, but it was just the two of us in the lecture hall.

"Is that so? Well, by all means," I say playfully. He smiles at me and I want to suck on those luscious lips again, but I hold back, for now anyway. He clears his throat and looks at me with a serious expression.

"What are your thoughts on the anal stage?" I almost want to laugh out loud at this, but I fix my face into a serious expression as well.

"Well, Mr Daniels, I would have to say that in my research, it is all about one's individual experience. It can either be unpleasant, or it can be a learning experience." I sit on my desk, and my skirt hikes up, something that Marcus immediately notices.

"Hm," he says thoughtfully, stroking my leg with his thumb. "I'm always up for learning experiences, Dr Anderson."

"Well, I think we should pick up where we left off with our first lesson, don't you think?" Without waiting for an answer, I grab him by the back of his head and kiss him on the lips forcefully. He groans and I feel him harden. I squirm in anticipation, pulling my skirt up a little more in order to spread my legs and wrap them around him. Marcus breaks the kiss and holds my face in his hands, a gleam in his eyes.

"You said where we left off...this isn't quite how we left off," he reminds me.

"Oh? Is that so?" I use his words teasingly. Eyeing the door one last time, I slide off my desk onto my feet. "Well if I remember correctly, this is where we left off." I graze the front of his pants with my nails and drop to my knees. Working fast, I unzip him and pull out that huge, magnificent cock. I can't help but admire it, then I lean over to take it into my mouth. Before my tongue could touch him, I pull back. I see his eyes widen, and I laugh. "Are you enjoying your lessons so far, Mr Daniels? As an educator, I want all my students to get as much out of my expertise as they can..."

"Hm. That's my plan too, professor." I smile and stroke his cock, leaning him against the wall for support. His quiet groans encourage me, and I pull his jeans all the way down and wrap my lips around him. I know it feels good because he grabs the back of my head tightly with both hands and pulls me all the way down. I gag and resist slightly, but he doesn't let up, he only slows his pace. He fucks my face for a good fifteen minutes; letting his balls slap me on the chin the whole time. I moan, wanting him to feel the vibration on his cock. He pulls me off him by my hair, making me yelp with the slight pain.

"What is it you were saying in your lecture earlier Dr Anderson? About the anal stage?"

"Another important developmental stage. I had said," I start, getting to my feet to come face to face with him. "It depends on everyone's experience. It's a learning experience," I whisper.

"Your thoughts?" he counters smoothly. I put my lips against his and reply in a mock shy voice, "I wouldn't know. I suppose this is where the student becomes the teacher?" In response, Marcus turns me around and pulls my skirt up. Pressing his cock against my panties, he leans over and whispers, "I learned from the best, Dr Anderson."

Using his member to push my panties aside, he bends me forward a little more and grabs my hips to steady himself. Without further ado, he begins to pound me from behind. He does it with so much brute force that I'm unable to even moan; I'm rendered speechless and breathless for a few good seconds. Catching my breath, I push back against him, matching his rhythm and forcing him deeper into me, and I feel him grab my long, light brown hair again, which I left in a ponytail, knowing how much he liked to play rough. I arch my back, making Marcus pump harder, and with his free hand, he takes his pinky finger to tease, then slowly insert into my ass, making me moan even louder at this completely new sensation. I feel my climax building, and apparently, Marcus does too, because he stops fingering my ass and simply leaves his finger in me as he pumps me even harder, if that's even possible. When I finally cum, I find myself gasping for air from the sheer force of it, and my whole body trembles and jerks with pleasure.

Marcus still hasn't cum, so I pull him out of me, and I look back at it, seeing his cock gleaming with my juices.

"Ready to teach, Mr Daniels?" I ask innocently, batting my eyes playfully.

"Always," he replies with a growl as he teases my ass with his still wet cock. He swirls it around, and I feel his precum lubing me as he barely penetrates me. I bite my lip in eagerness, impatient to feel him in me.

"Come on," I urge him. "I want to feel you, Marcus."

"You're definitely going to feel me, professor. You want my cock in your ass?"

"Yes…" I moan.

"Beg for it."

"Please…please…" I can barely get the words out of my mouth, now that he reaches around and slides his hands under my blouse and my bra. He expertly finds my nipples and tweaks them as I beg for him to fuck me.

"Please what?" he says calmly, tugging sharply on both nipples at the same time. I muffle a scream, knowing that there has to be people walking around right outside the door. Oddly enough, that thought makes my pussy throb, and I bite my lip again. "Please what?" he repeats, not letting up.

"Please fuck me," I beg.

"And who am I?" he probes, and I just know that he's standing over me smirking.

"Marcus…" I realize what it is that he wants, and I give it to him willingly. "Marcus, please fuck my ass." With that, he enters me in one fluid motion, which surprises me since it's my first time. It must be due to how wet we both are. He tries to start out slow and gentle, but I keep pushing back against him and he eventually quickens his pace until he starts to pound me again. He continues to pinch my nipples as he fucks me, and I hold onto the desk, which is shaking from the force of his thrusts. Try as I might, I moan loudly, unable to help myself, as I feel myself being stretched out for the first time.

"I'm going to cum in your ass, Dr Anderson. And you're going to walk around, feeling it drip out of your ass for the rest of the day," he informs me. I nod without thinking, and he grips me tight and suddenly goes still. I feel his cock twitch inside me and I feel my ass getting filled with his cum.

"Is it all in there?" I ask with a giggle as he pulls out slowly. And he's right, I do start to feel it drip out of me, and I kind of like the sensation and I hear Marcus laugh.

"So, professor, what's tomorrow's lecture going to be about?"

"You're just going to have to wait. Sit in on it tomorrow and learn, Mr Daniels," I wink, pulling my underwear up and my skirt down before I walk out of the lecture hall. "Hope to see you there. You have…potential." The last thing I see is his ever present smirk as I leave, excited for tomorrow's lecture already.

Chapter 5: Addicted

All things considered, there are worse things in the world than a college professor sleeping with her student. Especially when said student is tall, lean, and caramel with perfectly straight, white teeth and a thick, heavy cock. Just thinking about it makes my pussy throb, and here I am in the middle of traffic on a Tuesday morning. I screwed up this time, because I didn't even put together a coherent lesson plan, as I've been too busy either fucking Marcus or lazing around wishing I were fucking him. All I know is that we're studying different branches of childhood psychological development, which is easy enough to bullshit. I should be fine, I tell myself as I park across the street from the small college. Speed walking my way into the building, I make a beeline for my lecture hall and plop myself down, running a hand through my hair to steady myself as I try to think. Then, an idea comes to me and I sit back and smile, reading over my notes for the last fifteen minutes before my students are scheduled to come in.

I look up and smile warmly as the first few start to trickle in. All things considered, I do like my job very much. I get to go to different places, meet different people…and even interact with them. As if he senses my thoughts, Marcus walks in. In his dark blue nearly black jeans and dark gray turtleneck, he has the air of an intellectual.

"All right, good morning!" I greet everyone. "Today we're going to continue with Freud and look at his ideas about defense mechanisms. I know that most of you are freshmen, but is everyone familiar with this term?" Just about everyone nods, so I keep going. Not feeling like doing too much talking, I opt for a Socratic discussion today. "What are some of the most common defense mechanisms?" There's a pause, then three hands go up. I keep one eye on Marcus, who doesn't participate right away this time. I call on one dark skinned girl, who twists her lips, thinking of the word.

"I think it's called…repression?"

"Correct! And could you give us a definition of repression?" I urge her.

"Um, basically, it's when you bury painful memories so that you can cope with them." I nod and pose the next question to the rest of the class.

"Why would we need to do this?" And off we go in discussion. Surprisingly, Marcus stays silent during most of the discussion, though I do see him taking a few notes, so I know he's listening. We then segue into a discussion about frustration and overindulgence.

"But, Dr Anderson, overindulgence is just as bad as frustration, don't you think?" Marcus asks, raising his hand for the first time all day.

"Well, Mr Daniels, what do you think?" I counter. "Knowing what you know, do you think that it's just as bad to overindulge as it is to be deprived?" Everyone's eyes are on him, but his meet mine, and I feel the heat rise to my face and I have to avert my eyes briefly.

"Well," he repeats slowly, apparently choosing his words wisely. "If you keep denying yourself, or anyone else, something that they truly desire, that desire only becomes stronger. If it's not met, it becomes frustration, which would possibly lead to other problems in the subconscious. Or ego, I'm not sure which," he trails off, frowning down at his notes.

"Very good. But, I think what you're referring to is the superego. Still, that was very well explained." He gives a quick nod, and falls silent once more.

As I'm packing my things to go down to the cafeteria for break, I notice Marcus deliberately taking his time with his books. Waiting for the last student to leave, he looks back at the door, and then comes towards me slowly.

"Well, well. Marcus, you weren't too talkative today, what's wrong? You're usually the first one to participate," I say in a mock serious tone. He chuckles, then sits in the seat in front of me.

"Do you know what I was doing all morning before I came to school, Dr Anderson?" he ignores my question.

"What's that, Mr Daniels?"

"Remembering how tight and wet both your holes are," he replies bluntly. "And...wondering if they taste as good as they feel."

"Oh, really?" I ask, feigning shock. "Well, you know that curiosity killed the cat."

"Yes, I'm aware. However, he died knowing. So there's that." His smile is infectious, and I feel my knees getting weak as my pussy gets wet.

"In that case, kitty, I guess we'll both be satisfying our curiosity. Say, later in the afternoon? I have two more lectures in a little bit, but after that I'm all yours," I tell him seductively.

"I like the sound of that, professor," he licks his lips, and I can't help but wonder how they will feel on me. *I'll be finding out in a few hours!* I scream inside my head, a lascivious smile threatening to break through.

"Hm. I'll see you then," I dismiss him, not wanting anyone to come in unexpectedly. He stands up and struts out of the lecture hall, and I find myself licking my own lips, just as he did a moment ago.

Chapter 6: A Tease

I have no idea how the rest of his day went, but mine was a total bust. My next two lectures are on social psychology, and these are the more advanced students. I having them repeat themselves, lost in my own thoughts of Marcus, and anticipating the wonders that I'm almost positive that he can do with his tongue. Talk about frustration, I think to myself, hardly listening to one young man answer the question that I had just asked him thirty seconds ago. Luckily, all my lectures are only an hour long, so they all leave soon enough. Sighing and sitting back down behind my desk, I throw one leg on top of it and slip my hand into the waistband of my slacks. Pushing my hand further down, I finger the outline of my underwear, pushing it aside and insert one finger into my dripping pussy. Drawing the wetness out, I rub small circles around my clit, which is now sticking out from the hood, erect and firm. Closing my eyes and imagining Marcus' firm hand caressing me, I bring myself to a quick orgasm right there at my desk. Damn, I whisper, looking up to make sure nobody had seen me. Fixing my clothes, I stroll out of the room and to the cafeteria. Amid the buzz of students and professors talking, I grab a muffin and cappuccino and sit away from everyone.

"Hey there!" a deep, pleasant voice jolts me from my thoughts. I drop my muffin back onto the wax paper and nearly knock over my coffee, so deep in concentration am I.

"Oh, hi, Dr Whitman," I reply, steadying myself as I try to make myself somewhat presentable for the college's director.

"Enjoying your time here so far, Dr Anderson?" he asks, taking a seat next to me without me having offered, which puts me off a bit, but I let it slide.

"Um, yes. So far, so good. Why do you ask?" I reply, putting the cards on the table. I don't particularly like this man, but I do sort of work for him. Sort of. He clears his throat and doesn't quite meet my eyes when he talks to me.

"Just thought I'd ask, because something very interesting came to my attention yesterday."

"Oh?" my heart starts pounding, but I keep a blank expression on my face. "What was that?"

"A student in one of your lectures apparently has some interest in being a TA, Um, a Mr. Marcus Daniels. Do you know him?"

"Marcus Daniels? Yes, but isn't he a freshman? Which would mean that he couldn't qualify to be a TA, at least not anywhere that I know of."

"Actually, he's a transfer student. So technically, he's a sophomore, but with credits and such…you know how that goes." I nod, wanting Dr Whitman to get to the point already and get out of my face. "With that considered, I've seen his transcript from his previous school, and it's quite impressive, if I do say so myself. So he is, in fact, qualified to be a TA. And he insists on working with you. Ultimately, the decision is yours, but I just wanted to bring it to your attention." I take a calming sip of my cappuccino before replying, my mind racing for the right words.

"Well, Dr Whitman, understand that this is unusual because I go from institution to institution. That would compromise his education, so I think the best thing would be for me to perhaps recommend him to another colleague?" I suggest slowly. The director considers this for a moment, and then nods his assent.

"That would be great, Dr Anderson. Would you like to break the news to him, or should I?"

"No, no, that's fine. I'll do it. He'll be in my lecture on Thursday, I'll tell him then." I suppress a grin, and Dr Whitman excuses himself. Finally.

As Dr Whitman leaves, I catch a glimpse of a very familiar head of hair. I turn back to my coffee, finishing it off slowly, but looking back every so often out of the corner of my eye. When I'm done, I purposely pass by Marcus on my way to the trashcan. He is sitting with a few other students that I don't recognize.

"Mr Daniels," I greet him with am innocently friendly smile.

"Dr Anderson! Just the person I wanted to see," he exclaims, turning to his friends. "Hold on, I'll be back in a minute," He excuses himself and lowers his voice as he follows me to the trash.

"You applied to be a TA," I state, rather than ask. I can't help the biting tone in my voice, even though it's only because I'd had to deal with Dr Whitman.

"I did. Was that a bad thing?" he asks calmly.

"No, but it just caught me off guard. Why do you want to be a TA anyway?" I keep walking, and from the outside looking in, we appear to be a professor and her student in casual conversation.

"You do know that this is my major, so it could only help, for resume building and references…and, of course, the perks…" he trails off, leaving nothing to the imagination. I laugh as we turn down an empty hallway.

"Well if you want perks, you don't have to be my TA, you know," I stop and turn to wrap my arms around him. "See? Perks!" I slip my tongue into his mouth and he sucks gently on my bottom lip.

"Not here," he whispers against my lips, giving them a soft lick. "I know where we can go." He pulls me towards the stairs, and we run up three flights of stairs to the roof.

"The roof?" I ask incredulously once I see where we are.

"Yeah. Why?" he asks, laughing at my confused expression.

"A little cliché don't you think?" He smirks and pulls me in for another kiss, reaching for the front of my slacks at the same time.

"Why Mr Daniels, are you suggesting that we take our extracurricular activities outdoors today?"

"You damn right," he grunts as he gets my pants down over my hips. Kneeling on the ground, he throws both of my legs on either side of his face. My clit rests right on his nose and my pussy is smack dab on his lips, wet and very ready to be devoured. He sucks on both of my lips alternately, nibbling them the way he does to the ones on my face. I squirm, which allows him to nuzzle my clit. Tipping his head back, I feel him drag his tongue from my hole to my clit and back again, tracing circles and making me groan in frustration. "Hm. Someone's been naughty today," he chuckles, probably tasting my arousal from earlier.

"I'm naughty every day," I correct him, as I move my hips to grind my pussy harder onto his face. Encouraged by my statement, he sucks on my nub, as I cry out in ecstasy.

"I like the sound of that, Dr Anderson." Marcus thrusts his tongue deep into my pussy and I grab him by his thick, curly hair.

"And I like this," I moan, trying to keep as quiet as possible so that my voice won't echo. As Marcus fingers me, he barely touches me with the tip of his tongue, but as I reach my orgasm, he stops, leaving me with my chest heaving.

"You've already had your fun for today, professor," he says calmly, wiping his lips, both covered in my juices. "We'll leave the good stuff for next time." He grins and turns to leave me alone on the roof. Touché, Mr Daniels, touché, I utter under my breath.

Chapter 7: Dr. Whitman

The next day I'm technically supposed to be free, but I have to come by the school anyway. I always say that most institutions are nothing more than fancy cash cows, but I also believe in giving the devil his due. Therefore, I put on my best dark gray skirt suit and cream pumps. Brushing my hair into a knot on top of my head and dabbing some clear gloss on my lips, I make my way to school. Walking into the director's office, I see a few other people with him and my defenses automatically go up. Keeping a poker face on, I take a seat and try to feel them all out.

"Good morning," I say shortly, attempting a smile. Only one woman, with her hair back in a severe bun, smiles back; surely a bad sign.

"Dr Anderson," the director starts, frowning down at the papers on his desk. "Sorry to have to take you away from your day off, but this was the only convenient time for all of us. You understand." I force myself to not roll my eyes scathingly, and opt to not respond at all, hoping that they'll get on with it and let me go about my day.

"It seems that you've put in for another round here at this institution during the spring semester?" the woman with the bun asks.

"Um, yes, that's correct. A couple weeks in the spring, I'd like to give more lectures."

"Were you, perhaps, hoping for a permanent position here?" one of the men asks with a poorly disguised sneer. I raise an eyebrow, forgetting about my poker face, and his sneer turns into a small grin.

"No," I begin slowly. "That was not my intention at all. Why, are you offering?" I shoot back. Dr Whitman raises a hand to silence us.

"Dr Anderson, that won't be necessary. We have a well-documented file on you for your time here, as well as your references. We will be informing you of our decision by the end of next week."

"But…what? These things don't usually go before review boards, Dr Whitman. Why now?"

"Thank you, Dr Anderson," he dismisses me without so much as a glance. The others leave, and the sneering man now has an openly gloating look on his face. As they leave, I stand up, pulling my skirt back down over my knees. I was so deep in thought that I don't realize that Dr Whitman is right behind me until I accidentally step on his wing tipped shoe.

"I apologize, Dr Whitman," I say shortly, stepping away from him to leave. "Good bye." Before I turn around, he grabs me forcefully by my wrist, causing me to cry out in pain. "Dr Whitman!" I yell.

"You want this job, don't you, Dr Anderson?" he breathes.

"What?!" I try to pull my wrist away, to no avail. "Let go of me! Right now!"

"You're right, these things usually don't go before the review board," he pulls me to him and his mouth is against my ear. I can feel his wet breath as he speaks, and it makes me nauseous. "But what you don't know is that I am the review board…I make the ultimate decision, not the other pricks." Getting over the initial shock, I finally wrench my arm from his grip and spit in his face.

"Go fuck yourself, Dr Whitman. Fuck this place, too. I don't need this." I turn to storm out of the office, and then turn back to him. "By the way, if you even think of blackballing me or denying me a reference…well, I don't think I need to explain to you what a sexual harassment charge would do to you, do I?"

"You wouldn't dare," he growls, peering at me through squinted eyes.

"Don't dare me," I threaten. "You don't want to test me on this." Rushing out, I stride blindly into the hallway, not really having any place to go. I'm near tears, but they don't fall; I'm simply too infuriated to cry. Turning a corner, I run face first into Marcus. Stumbling back, I realize I'm out of breath.

"Dr Anderson!" he looks at me, wide eyed, and I can't imagine how I must look. "Did I miss your lecture today?"

"N-no, Mr Daniels. I, uh, didn't have any lecture today. I came for a staff meeting." Why am I explaining any of this to him? I ask myself.

"Oh, okay. Well, are you all right?" he asks with a frown. Two girls come around the corner, and he quickly changes tack. "I had some questions about the last lecture? It also pertains to my 102 class, so I figured I'd go ahead and ask." Grateful for the distraction, I allow him to lead me down the hall.

"Sure, Mr Daniels," I tell him as we walk. "We can go over it in the cafeteria if you have a minute?" Lowering his voice as we approach another group of students, he shakes his head as he replies, "I was thinking of someplace a little quieter."

Chapter 8: Once You Go Black....

For a young guy in a big city, or really anywhere, Marcus does pretty well for himself. He has a small studio not too far from the college, and even though he doesn't have extravagant furniture, everything is tidy and impeccably clean. Sighing, I come out with what I've had on my mind the whole trip over here.

"Marcus, I'm leaving the campus. So you definitely won't be my TA."

"Oh?" he asks in surprise, stopping in his tracks. "Any particular reason why?" he tries to sound casual but fails miserably, and I laugh for the first time all day.

"None that I care to share at the moment," I answer, throwing my arms around him and silencing him with a sound kiss.

"Hm. And have you been a good girl?" he inquires, reaching down to give my ass a hard squeeze. I moan happily and giggle.

"Umm...so far today, yeah. But I'd like to change that, if we can?" I look up at him as innocently as I can, and lick my lower lip. Without missing a beat, Marcus swipes his finger across it, then sticks his finger into his mouth and I begin sucking on it sensually.

"You do realize that I never finished tasting you, right?" He unbuttons my blouse and kisses me in the spot in between my breasts, making me fidget a little from the ticklish sensation.

"I know. In fact, I believe you owe me one from yesterday, if I remember correctly?"

"You're absolutely right, professor." He nuzzles my breasts, kissing underneath them and leaving small bite marks as he goes, which I don't mind. Without stopping, he pushes me gently towards his kitchen counter, then lifts me up effortlessly to sit me on top of it. I settle onto the Formica counter, my skirt hiking up nearly to my hips. "Perfect," he whispers as he pushes my underwear aside. Closing my eyes, I feel his tongue parting my pussy lips, and I unwittingly hold my breath. Feeling the long, languid strokes of his tongue, I want to cum but I hold back, gritting my teeth with the effort. Reaching down, I hold my lips apart for him, and he inserts two fingers before sucking on my clit like a lollipop.

Leaning my head against a cabinet, I grab him by his hair again, holding him in place. Surprising me, he concentrates on my clit with his tongue, but takes his fingers out of my pussy and carefully slides one into my ass. I push my hips up to meet him, driving his finger deeper and I feel myself on the verge of a great orgasm.

"Mmm Marcus...I'm about to cum," I whimper. He begins to finger me harder, and with a sharp cry, I feel my release. "Oh, God, yes." Letting go of my clit, I see him lick his lips, savoring my taste.

"Looks like I was wrong. You taste much better than I imagined...Dr Anderson." I giggle, wrapping my legs around his neck.

"Are you sure? Maybe you need another taste." He lifts my hips slightly, trying to get to my ass. Failing at that, he pushes my legs up so that they form a perfect V. In this position, he is able to tease and probe my asshole, but I can't move my hips to meet his tongue. Marcus licks off whatever remaining cum is dripping out of my slit, then spreads it on my asshole with his tongue.

"Your asshole tastes good to me," he murmurs, barely penetrating me with the tip of his tongue. "But, I have someone that needs some attention, too."

"By all means," I spread my legs even wider, giving him better access to my tight hole. He drops his pants and I notice his cock is already dripping precum. I wonder to myself how long he's been holding back, and how long it would take for him to explode. Guess we'll find out, I tell myself excitedly, waiting for him to slip me that thick, throbbing rod. After a moment, I notice that he's having a little trouble. "Come on," I urge him teasingly. "Give me that cock, Mr Daniels." He gives me a mock sneer and reaches for a small bottle of olive oil, and pours a little bit into his palm. He strokes himself with his oiled hand, making his cock glisten under the kitchen light, then rubs some on my asshole. The warmth of the oil is inviting and serves to excite me more.

Marcus penetrates me with ease, holding my legs up in the air as he slowly pumps my ass. Feeling how smoothly he can fuck me, due to the olive oil, he starts to fuck me harder, making me grab the counter to keep my balance.

"Yes…yes…fuck me harder, Marcus!" I cry out, not caring about the noise. We're finally alone, so I take full advantage.

"Who knew my professor would be such a little slut," he grunts, tightening his grip on my legs.

"I'll show you a slut, Mr Daniels," I reply saucily, and he raises an eyebrow at this. "When you cum, pull out and cum on my tits so I can clean you off," I whisper, feeling sweat break out on my forehead.

"Oh, so you want to be my cum whore now?" he asks, pounding me furiously. I grit my teeth, as it's starting to hurt a bit, but I manage to take it.

"That's right. Give me that cum, daddy." Marcus pulls his cock out of me, making me jerk with the unexpected tug, and I squeeze my breasts together, waiting for him to cum. Holding the base, he aims for my breasts and shoots a thick load on them. Spurt after spurt hits me, and I rub it in before it drips too much. Smiling seductively into his eyes, I bend over and take his cock in my mouth before it can completely soften. Sucking softly, I make sure he's totally clean, and I even enjoy my taste mixed with his.

"Are you going to tell me what happened now?" Marcus asks after we both catch our breath.

"Eh. I'm not too worried about it. It's not a big deal anyway," I brush him off, not wanting to spoil my good mood. "You'll still be able to have your…extracurricular activities with me."

Bonus Sample:

FORBIDDEN PLEASURES

Begging My Professor For The A

My Naughty Backdoor Fantasy

Everlette Saunders

Table Of Contents

Chapter 1: Leanna & Johnny

"That's exactly what I want Johnny, Oh yes... yes."
Leanna quickly covered her hand with her mouth as
she looked down to watch her boyfriend's head moving
vigorously between her thighs.

Normally she wouldn't care, being loud was part of the
fun, and she liked to express herself, but tonight they were at
a frat party, and as much as she would love to make sure
everyone knew what was happening in the laundry room, she
needed to find release more. She was currently leaning back
on the washing machine with one foot planted on the top and
the other hanging down. She was resting on her elbows so
that should watch his head moving. She loved to watch him in
action. She felt his fingers probing her roughly. Gone was any
idea of being soft or careful. She was wet, swollen and aching.
Johnny was always such a giver and she loved getting him
riled up. It all started when they first arrived at the party.

They always played this game where they would pick
out the hottest woman in the room and talk about who would
have her first, and how. Tonight had been a beautiful blonde.
Petite in the waist with huge breasts, she had been the perfect
one to point out to him. She knew he always liked a woman
with a nice rack. He immediately chimed in as they played out
the fantasy verbally. They had both been hot and ready when
they found their way to this room. There were slits in the folds
in the door so anyone could see if they happened to pass by,
part of the thrill for her. Johnny had described how much he
wanted to pump into both her and the little blonde over and
over, back and forth between the two. Thinking of it again now
pushed her over the edge and into the sweet oblivion that she
needed.

"That's it don't you stop Johnny, side to side, yes yes."
She moaned loudly, grinding into his face as the wave
hit her.

He knew her body well enough to know she was sated and immediately pulled her, scooting her forward until she was slightly hanging off of the machine. He moved and pushed into her roughly, slamming and banging. She loved the roughness and always wanted more, but Johnny wasn't as into it as she was. She laid flat on her back to give him better access and she moaned as she felt him deeper than before. He was average in size, but he made up for it in his eagerness to please.

She felt him push into her longer and slower and she knew he was nearing release. This was the best time to ask for what she really wanted.

"Johnny baby, take me the other way, the way I really want." She begged him, knowing he loved when she begged. He looked up at her and swore as he found release. When it was over he smiled at her.

"You're so good baby, I love when you beg I can't help it... besides we've talked about that. You know how I feel about it, it's just not something I'm into." He helped her stand and gave her a kiss. She kissed him back.

CPSIA information can be obtained
at www.ICGtesting.com
Printed in the USA
BVHW051748050623
665420BV00029B/567

9 781512 297614